088994

M   Murphy, Jim
           Backyard bear.

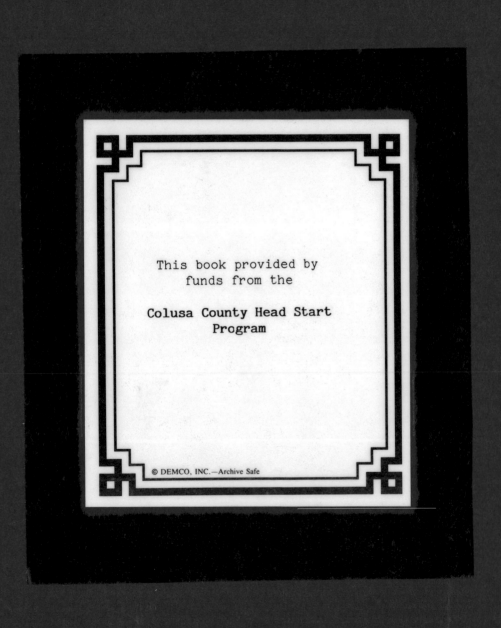

This book provided by
funds from the

**Colusa County Head Start
Program**

BACKYARD BEAR

by JIM MURPHY • Illustrated by JEFFREY GREENE

SCHOLASTIC
HARDCOVER

SCHOLASTIC INC.
New York

Library of Congress Cataloging-in-Publication Data

Murphy, Jim, 1947-
Backyard bear / by Jim Murphy; illustrated by Jeffrey Greene.
p.   cm.
Includes bibliographical references (p 32).
Summary: After developers encroach upon its forest home, a young
black bear wanders into a neighborhood and creates chaos in the
middle of a peaceful summer night.
ISBN 0-590-44375-5
1. Black bear — Juvenile fiction. [1. Black bear — Fiction.
2. Bears — Fiction.] I. Greene, Jeffrey, ill. II. Title.
PZ10.3.M953Bac   1992
[E] — dc20   92-15479
CIP
AC

12 11 10 9 8 7 6 5 4 3 2 1   3 4 5 6 7/9

Printed in the U.S.A.   37

First Scholastic printing, February 1993

Book design by David Turner

The illustrations in this book
were done in pastel

For Nonni and Al — city slickers on the
outside, but wild at heart.
— J.M.

For Dorothy and Harry,
and especially for Bob.
— J.G.

THE YOUNG black bear trots along the dark path, sniffing the night air for food. The smell of blackberries is so thick he can almost taste them.

He comes around a bend in the path and stops. Too late. An older, bigger bear is already tugging berries from the bush and shoving them into his mouth. When the young bear steps toward the berries, the other bear snaps his teeth and growls. *Stay clear,* he warns. *These are mine.*

The blackberries are so close and the young bear is so hungry. Slowly, he inches toward the berries. He reaches out a paw. . . .

The older bear lunges, teeth and claws ready. A massive paw flashes at the young bear. Before the paw can strike, he ducks, turns, and begins running. In terror he crashes through the forest and does not stop until he's sure the other bear is not after him.

Exhausted and panting, the young bear finds himself standing at the top of a mountain. It's then that he smells food again. He sniffs to be sure it isn't the blackberries. No, this is different. It's close by, too, somewhere in the town below. The bear scratches his ear, then moves toward the smell.

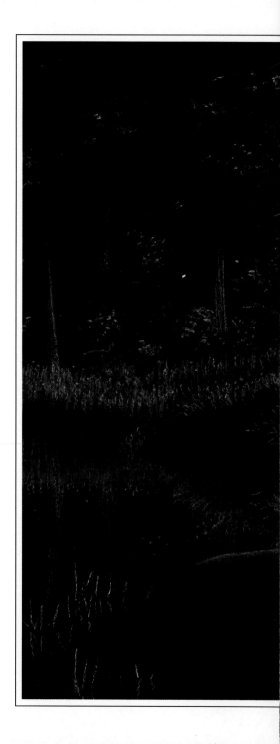

At the bottom of the mountain, he pauses. A ribbon of asphalt separates his forest from their town. To cross the road is to trespass.

The wind shifts and the delicious smell of food surrounds him. The houses look strange, all dark hard lines. But at least no older bears are down there to chase him. A second later, he crosses the road and enters the sleeping town.

As soon as he walks between two houses he feels closed in by the walls. The concrete driveway is hard and scratchy.

He comes to a backyard. Shirts and pants flap on a clothesline. A barbecue grill stands next to a wooden chair. Nothing looks right. Nothing reminds him of his forest. Only the smell of food is familiar.

There is movement in the next yard. What is it? He looks into the darkness, sniffing. Some animal is after his food. The bear hurries across the yard.

He sees a mother raccoon and her three babies. They weave their way around a baseball bat and glove, an army helmet, toy soldiers, a bicycle.

The bear follows them, inching past a wooden fort. As he does, his shadow stretches out until it touches the raccoons. The mother raccoon spins to defend her children, hissing loudly.

The bear doesn't want to fight. All he wants is his food. He steps away from the raccoons and bumps into the fort. The next instant, the walls of the fort come crashing down.

The noise frightens the raccoons and they run off. But the bear stands, too scared to move. A dog inside the house begins barking.

The dog leaps against the back door to get out, its barking loud and angry. The bear scurries to the darkest corner of the yard just as the back door opens. Two people stick their heads out.

"Can't see a thing," the man says, holding the dog by its collar. "Settle down, Caesar. There's nothing out there."

"I heard something," the woman says. "So did Caesar. Let's check."

"Okay, okay," the man mutters. "But it's probably nothing." The porch light pops on and the bear moves deeper into the shadows.

The man and the woman come out onto the porch. "I still can't see anything," he says while the dog strains to break free. "Wish I had my glasses."

The bear doesn't like these animals or the nervous sounds they are making. He especially doesn't like the angry dog. He notices a space between two garages, enters it, and runs until he comes to a fence.

"There!" the woman says. "Something moved."

A boy appears at a window. "Hey, what's going on?"

"Some animal's in the backyard," his father answers.

"Neat!" the boy says. "I'll get the flashlight. And my camera."

"And I'll call the police," the mother says. "You never know. It could be dangerous."

The woman returns a moment later. "They'll be here soon," she says. "Has it moved?"

"No," says the father. "Probably just someone's dog."

"I've never seen a dog *that* big," the woman insists.

The boy arrives and gives his mother the flashlight. She flicks it on and a beam of light probes the night. They all head for the garage.

"Up here," the man whispers as Caesar drags him forward.

"Don't do anything until I get a picture," the boy tells his parents.

The woman shines the flashlight between the garages. The bear tries to back away but thumps into the fence, trapped. Just then light hits him in the face.

"A bear!" the man says.

The boy points his camera at the bear. "Get out of the way, Mom."

A police car screeches into the driveway and two policemen leap out.

"In here, in here," the woman calls out, pointing. "It's a bear."

More animals and more sounds to block his escape. The bear doesn't like this. He shakes his head, snapping his teeth several times.

The policemen aim their emergency lights at the bear. The lights sting the bear's eyes and he has to blink to see. He stands up on his hind legs, waving his paws.

"It's going to attack," the man yells. Caesar breaks loose and rushes at the bear.

The dog leaps, his teeth bared, but the bear is bigger and quicker. With one swat, he sends the dog flying against the side of the garage.

"Caesar! No!" The woman grabs his collar before he can charge again. "Down boy, down."

"Get back!" a policeman orders. "Get back!" He pulls his gun and is about to shoot when the boy's camera flash goes off. The explosion of light startles the bear and makes him turn away. The bear is so big and strong he knocks the fence over.

An open space welcomes the bear. Without any hesitation he runs across the yard, pulling down a line of clothes as he escapes.

"He's getting away," the woman shouts. "Shoot him."

"It's too dark," a policeman says. "Let's call in some help."

The bear hears loud shouting, but doesn't stop. He keeps on running from yard to yard. Every time he sees a dark area of shadow, he heads for it. Finally, he comes to a huge shrub beside a house.

He can hear sirens. Being near the house makes him nervous, but he needs to rest. He pushes his way inside the shrub. It is cool and dark and quiet in here. And safe. He curls up in a tight ball.

Suddenly, noise surrounds him again. Sirens wailing, people shouting. Flashlights search the darkness for him. The bear's muscles stiffen, ready to fight.

"Think he came this way?" one policeman asks. "Keep your gun ready."

"A guy said it ran through here," the other replies. "But he was pretty shook up. Probably his imagination."

The policemen walk past the shrub but do not look inside it.

The bear watches their dark shapes disappear between two houses. He relaxes, but does not move. Instead, he watches and listens for many hours.

Gradually, the sky begins to brighten. The bear has not seen or heard anything for a very long time.

He is about to step out of the shrub when a car turns down the street. A rolled-up newspaper flies from its window. The bear watches as the car goes past and then the street is quiet again.

The bear stares at the newspaper. It does not move or threaten him. When he feels safe, the bear hurries around the paper, crosses the road, and enters the forest.

He remembers the big bear trying to hit him, and pauses. Still, the dark shapes and noise and lights and dog seem even scarier now. At least in the forest he is surrounded by familiar things. And somewhere in the woods he'll find a territory of his own. And food. His claws dig into the dirt as his big legs carry him up the mountain to find his new home.

The Bear Facts

The newspaper headline was printed in large, bold type that screamed: YOUNG BEARS ARE COMING! Such news might not be so unusual in rural areas. But this particular headline appeared in the paper of a densely populated New Jersey town not far from New York City. Similar warnings are being issued in hundreds of other suburbs and cities all across the United States.

"One- and two-year-old black bears are being forced out of their home territories by older males," explains Richard Henry, a bear expert for the New York Department of Environmental Conservation. "That's normal. It's always happened that way. The trouble is that there isn't much undeveloped space left anymore, so they end up wandering into nearby towns."

A representative for the Humane Society in Pasadena, California, says, "If we would stop encroaching into their territory, they would stop coming into ours. Since that's not going to happen, all we can do is try to educate people about the bears and hope for the best."

Black bears live throughout the United States and Canada. A small number can even be found in parts of Mexico. They are large and powerful animals, with adult females capable of weighing 350 pounds and the males up to 750 pounds. Despite their size, bears are surprisingly agile and fast. Recently, animal biologists clocked a running bear at 33 miles per hour — that's faster than any human can run.

"They also have a terrific sense of smell," a spokesman for the Illinois Wildlife Department notes. "They can detect food miles away and then locate it. And they're smart, too. They know that garbage dumps and garbage pails are handy sources of food. Hey, why should they run all around and get tired hunting for a meal when they know where to get fast food."

Fortunately, most of us will never have a face-to-face encounter with a black bear. They are nocturnal creatures, so while they are out prowling for food most of us are safe in bed. And for the most part they tend to be afraid of humans and will avoid contact at all costs. Gary Alt, of the Pennsylvania Game Commission, states, "I honestly consider the domestic dog a more serious threat to humans than the black bear." Alt notes that trouble usually develops when a bear grows accustomed to feeding on garbage.

"These bears have very little fear of humans," says Louis Berchielli, from the New York Department of Environmental Conservation. "They expect to walk into a backyard and eat the garbage without any interference."

What should you do if you happen to bump into a bear? Experts offer a few simple suggestions. First, back away slowly and then stay as far from the bear as possible. Next, notify the local police department and wildlife associations.

"The real culprit is the people," says the director of the California Wildlife Defenders. She complains that too many people see bears as big, cuddly toys. "They want to get close to them, feed them or get pictures of them to show their friends."

The most important thing to remember about a black bear is that it is a *wild* animal with sharp claws and sharp teeth. A crowd of people closing in around it might make it nervous enough to attack, especially if it sees no obvious way to escape.

"So far, we've had no problems with bears and people," Mr. Berchielli says. "But the closer people and bears get, the greater is the potential for a confrontation." Mr. Berchielli adds, "Bears and people can coexist. All we have to do is use care and a little common sense. If we do our part, the bears will do theirs and we'll all live happily and safely. It's not hard at all really."

Finding Out More About Bears

Below you will find a brief list of sources of information about black bears, most illustrated with photographs. Many of these books have been published by state wildlife agencies. You might want to contact your own state agencies for any information they might have on bears in your area. In addition, check the magazine section of your school or public library. Most conservation and wildlife magazines have done articles about this remarkable animal.

Burk, Dale, ed. *The Black Bear in Modern North America.* Clinton, New Jersey: Boone and Crockett Club and Amwell Press, 1979.

Cardoza, James E. *The History and Status of the Black Bear in the New England States.* Westborough: Massachusetts Division of Fisheries and Wildlife, 1976.

East, Ben. *Bears.* New York: Outdoor Life – Times Mirror, Inc., 1977.

Ford, Barbara. *Black Bear: The Spirit of the Wilderness.* Boston: Houghton Mifflin Co., 1981.

Hopkins, David M., Mathews, John V., Schweger, Charles E., and Young, Steven B. *Paleoecology of Beringia.* New York: Academic Press, 1982.

Poelker, Richard J., and Hartwell, Harry D. *Black Bear of Washington.* Washington: Washington State Game Department, 1973.

Tyler, Hamilton A. *Pueblo Animals and Myths.* Norman: University of Oklahoma Press, 1975.

Van Wormer, Joe. *World of the Black Bear.* Philadelphia: J. B. Lippincott, 1966.

Whitaker, John O. *The Audubon Society Field to North American Mammals.* New York: Alfred A. Knopf, 1980.

Willey, Charles H. *The Vermont Black Bear.* Montpelier: Vermont Fish and Game Department, 1978.